# A Note to Parents

Welcome to REAL KIDS READERS, a series of phonics-based books for children who are beginning to read. In the classroom, educators use phonics to teach children how to sound out unfamiliar words, providing a firm foundation for reading skills. At home, you can use REAL KIDS READERS to reinforce and build on that foundation, because the books follow the same basic phonic guidelines that children learn in school.

Of course the best way to help your child become a good reader is to make the experience fun—and REAL KIDS READERS do that, too. With their realistic story lines and lively characters, the books engage children's imaginations. With their clean design and sparkling photographs, they provide picture clues that help new readers decipher the text. The combination is sure to entertain young children and make them truly want to read.

REAL KIDS READERS have been developed at three distinct levels to make it easy for children to read at their own pace.

- LEVEL 1 is for children who are just beginning to read.
- LEVEL 2 is for children who can read with help.
- LEVEL 3 is for children who can read on their own.

A controlled vocabulary provides the framework at each level. Repetition, rhyme, and humor help increase word skills. Because children can understand the words and follow the stories, they quickly develop confidence. They go back to each book again and again, increasing their proficiency and sense of accomplishment, until they're ready to move on to the next level. The result is a rich and rewarding experience that will help them develop a lifelong love of reading.

Produced by DWAI/Seventeenth Street Productions, Inc.

*Library of Congress Cataloging-in-Publication Data*

Venn, Cecilia.
    On with the show! / by Cecilia Venn ; photography by Dorothy Handelman.
        p.       cm. — (Real kids readers. Level 3)
    Summary: While babysitting, Lisa, Beth, Nick, and Max organize a show to celebrate Clean
Up Pocket Park Day.
    ISBN 0-7613-2011-3 (lib. bdg.). — ISBN 0-7613-2036-9 (pbk.)
    [1. Litter (Trash)—Fiction. 2. Babysitters—Fiction.] I. Handelman, Dorothy, ill. II. Title.
III. Series.
PZ7.V558On   1998
[Fic]—dc21                                                                          97-31369
                                                                                    CIP
                                                                                    AC

                        pbk: 10 9 8 7 6 5 4 3 2
                        lib:  10 9 8 7 6 5 4 3 2

# On with the Show!

## Cecilia Venn

Photographs by **Dorothy Handelman**

## The Millbrook Press
### Brookfield, Connecticut

It was Saturday morning. Beth, Nick, and Max went to Pocket Park to meet their friend Lisa. The park was small, with houses on the sides and a gate at each end. Usually it was the kids' favorite place. But today it was a mess.

"Yuck!" said Beth. "Look at this." She picked up an old brown bag lying by the gate.

"Let's move the trash can closer to the gate," said Nick. "Then maybe people won't litter." He took one side of the can and Max took the other. They started walking, but suddenly something rolled under their feet.

"Look out!" cried Beth.

Too late! Max tripped and fell, taking the can with him. Trash spilled everywhere. A newspaper even landed on Nick's head.

"Nice hat," said Beth.

Max stood up. A banana peel slid down his leg. He kicked a red-and-white ball out of his way. "Where did that come from?" he asked.

"Hi, everybody!" It was Lisa, pulling her sister Jenna in a wagon.

"My ball!" said Jenna.

"Nice throw," said Beth.

"Uh-oh," said Lisa. "Sorry, guys."

Lisa helped the others pick up the mess. "Good thing today is Clean Up Pocket Park Day," she said.

"What do you mean?" asked Nick.

"The grownups plan to clean up the park," said Lisa. "See them over in our backyard? They're having a meeting about it. That's why I'm watching Jenna."

"I know what they should do first," said Max. "They should clean up that big pile of dirt by the fence."

"That dirt is for a new garden," said Lisa.

"I hope they don't plant peas," Max said. "Yuck!"

Lisa pulled the wagon over to a park bench. Nick and Max sat down, but Beth walked back and forth. She was working on an idea.

"Everyone needs to think more about keeping the park clean," she said. "So why don't we put on a show about trash?"

"Good idea!" said Nick and Max.

"Yes—only I have to watch Jenna," said Lisa.

"Don't worry, we'll help," said Beth. "There are four of us. How hard could it be to watch one little girl?"

Beth ran home and got a broom. She swept a spot clean. "Let's put on the show right here," she said. "We can use the bench for seating."

"Look, Jenna," said Lisa. "You have a front row seat!"

Jenna smiled and clapped her hands.

"On with the show!" said Beth.

While Beth was sweeping, Nick had gone home. Now he was back, carrying a big box.

"Could we use any of this?" he asked. He turned the box upside down. All kinds of art stuff spilled out in a heap.

Lisa pulled out some long, colorful ribbons. "I could do a dance with these," she said. "I could show how the wind blows trash around."

Max picked out a roll of tinfoil. "I'm going to wrap myself in this and be a dancing trash can," he said. "There's enough for you too, Beth."

Beth looked at Max. She looked at Lisa. "I want to be the wind," she said.

Lisa found some more ribbons and handed them to Beth. Then she went to check on Jenna.

The wagon was empty.

"Oh, no!" cried Lisa. "Where's Jenna?"

Everybody stopped and looked around. No Jenna!

*Thump! Thump! Thump!*

"What's that?" asked Max.

"Look! My box is moving," Nick said. He tipped over the box.

"Peekaboo," said Jenna.

Lisa sighed. "Come with me, Jenna," she said. "You can watch our dance."

"Just do what I do," Lisa told Beth. She waved her ribbons from side to side. So did Beth. She spun on her toes. So did Beth. But this time the ribbons did not move.

"*Whoa!*" the girls cried.

Max and Nick laughed. "You may be the wind," said Max. "But you're not blowing very hard."

"I'm ready to blow my top," said Beth. "Could you please watch Jenna? We have to sort out our ribbons."

Max took Jenna's hand and led her back to the bench. "Watch this," he said. "I'm going to turn into a trash can."

He pulled out a long sheet of foil and put it on the ground. Then he lay down on top of it and grabbed one end.

"Check this out, Jenna!" he called. He rolled over and over. The foil wrapped around and around.

"Uh-oh!" said Max. "Help!"

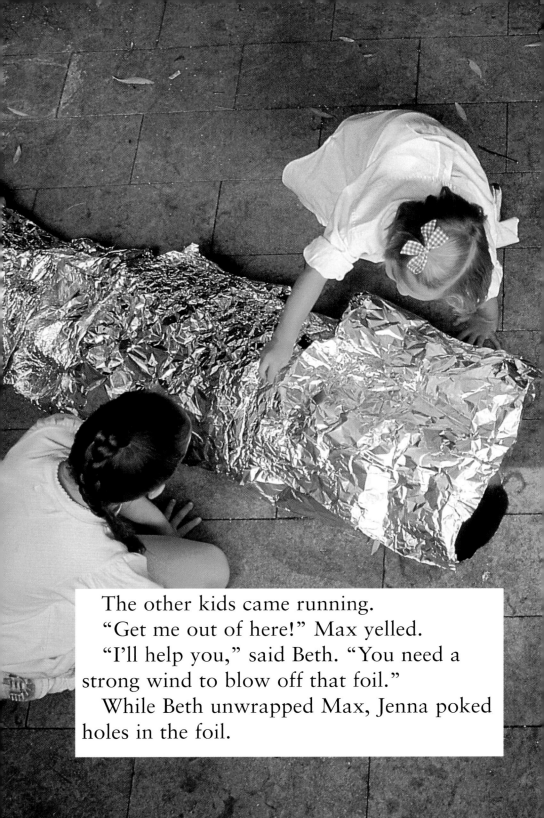

The other kids came running.

"Get me out of here!" Max yelled.

"I'll help you," said Beth. "You need a strong wind to blow off that foil."

While Beth unwrapped Max, Jenna poked holes in the foil.

"Jenna sure gets in the way," said Lisa. "Maybe we should go home."

"Nooooo!" Jenna cried.

"Lisa, are you two okay?" Lisa's mom called from the yard.

"We're fine, Mom," Lisa called back. She turned to her sister. "Jenna, hush!" she said. "Okay, we'll stay."

Lisa and Beth went back to dancing.
This time they gave Jenna her own ribbons.

Nick taped the top of his box shut.

"What are you making?" Max asked him.

"A trash eater," Nick said.

Max was not sure what Nick meant, but it sounded good. "Can I help?" he asked.

"Sure," Nick said.

Nick cut a big round hole in the box. "This is the mouth," he told Max. "All the trash goes in here."

Max drew sharp teeth around the hole.

"Let's paint this trash eater," said Nick.

"Let's put it on wheels!" said Max. "You start painting. I'll go home and get my skateboard."

Nick opened the paints. He gave the trash eater a red nose and blue eyes.

Max came back with his skateboard. "Looks good," he told Nick.

"Hey, guys!" Beth and Lisa called. "Come and see our dance."

Nick and Max went to watch the girls. Suddenly they heard some funny noises behind them. *Thump! Splat! Splash!*

They ran back to the trash eater. Jenna was throwing paint cans into its mouth!

"Trash!" said Jenna.

Lisa came over and pulled her sister away from the box. Jenna was covered with paint.

"Oh, Jenna," she said. "You are such a mess! How will I ever clean you up?"

"I'll go get soap and water," said Max. He went home and got a big bar of soap and a small bucket of water. But as he ran back to Jenna, he tripped.

Water splashed all over Jenna's shirt.
"Uh-oh," Max said.
Jenna started to yell.

"Lisa, what is going on?" her mom called.

"Nothing," Lisa called back. She turned to Beth. "Do you know how hard it can be to watch one little girl?" she asked.

"How hard?" said Beth.

"Very hard!" said Lisa.

Max put a piece of foil on the ground. "Put Jenna's shirt on this," he said. "The sun will heat the foil and help dry the shirt."

Lisa took Jenna's shirt off and put it on the foil. "Whew! I need a rest," she said.

"I want a snack," Jenna said.

"Wait here," Max said. He headed home—again.

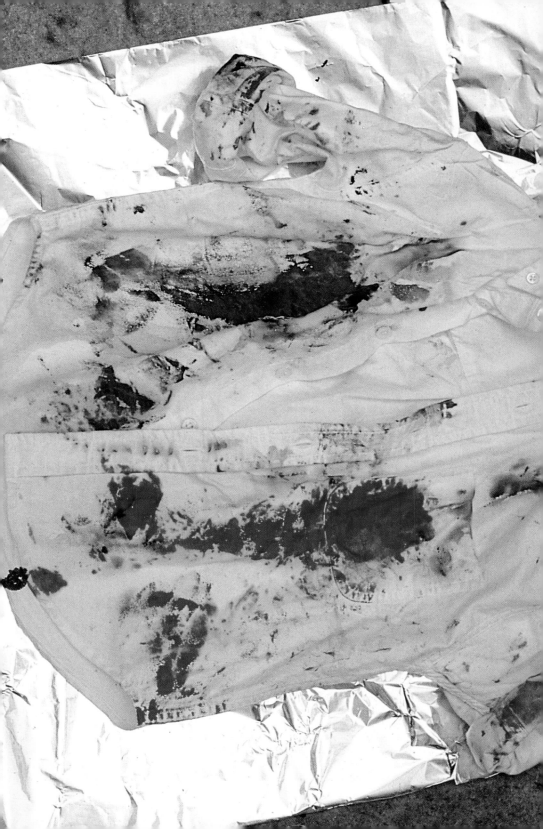

Max came back with a brown bag. "I hope you all like peanut butter and jelly," he said.

"Yum!" said Nick and Beth and Lisa. The big kids ate and talked about the show. Jenna just ate. "All done," she said.

Lisa took Jenna's ribbon. She tried to clean her sister's face and hands. But there were still spots of paint and jelly left.

"Let's get back to work," said Beth.

"What about Jenna?" Lisa asked. "We better give her something to do."

Everybody looked at the little girl.

"I have an idea," said Max. He went over to the big pile of dirt. He filled the small pail and came back. Then he took some foil and folded it into a scoop.

"Here you go," he said to Jenna. "Now you have a job too."

Jenna smiled. She picked up the foil scoop.

"Ta-da!" said Max.

Then Jenna picked up the pail of dirt and dumped it all out—into her lap!

Max laughed. So did Beth and Nick. Even Lisa joined in.

"Jenna, you are the biggest mess in Pocket Park," said Max.

"That gives me an idea," said Beth. "Quick! Get the wagon. Let's make a float!"

"Here come the grownups," said Nick.
"Are you ready?" said Beth.
"Ready," said Nick and Max and Lisa.
"Then let's go!" cried Beth. "On with the show!"

Beth danced out with her streamers. Nick pushed the trash eater. Max skipped along beside him. And Lisa pulled the float. In it sat Jenna—covered with paint and dirt. She was waving a bar of soap.

Clean Up Pocket Park Day was on!

# Reading with Your Child

Even though your child is reading more independently now, it is vital that you continue to take part in this important learning experience.

- Try to read with your child at least twenty minutes each day, as part of your regular routine.
- Encourage your child to keep favorite books in one convenient, cozy spot, so you don't waste valuable reading time looking for them.
- Read and familiarize yourself with the Phonic Guidelines on the next pages.
- Praise your young reader. Be the cheerleader, not the teacher. Your enthusiasm and encouragement are key ingredients in your child's success.

## What to Do if Your Child Gets Stuck on a Word

- Wait a moment to see if he or she works it out alone.
- Help him or her decode the word phonetically. Say, "Try to sound it out."
- Encourage him or her to use picture clues. Say, "What does the picture show?"
- Encourage him or her to use context clues. Say, "What would make sense?"
- Ask him or her to try again. Say, "Read the sentence again and start the tricky word. Get your mouth ready to say it."
- If your child still doesn't "get" the word, tell him or her what it is. Don't wait for frustration to build.

## What to Do if Your Child Makes a Mistake

- If the mistake makes sense, ignore it—unless it is part of a pattern of errors you wish to correct.
- If the mistake doesn't make sense, wait a moment to see if your child corrects it.
- If your child doesn't correct the mistake, ask him or her to try again, either by decoding the word or by using context or picture clues. Say, "Get your mouth ready" or "Make it sound right" or "Make it make sense."
- If your child still doesn't "get" the word, tell him or her what it is. Don't wait for frustration to build.

# Phonic Guidelines

Use the following guidelines to help your child read the words in this story.

## Short Vowels
When two consonants surround a vowel, the sound of the vowel is usually short. This means you pronounce *a* as in apple, *e* as in egg, *i* as in igloo, *o* as in octopus, and *u* as in umbrella. Words with short vowels include: *bed, big, box, cat, cup, dad, dog, get, hid, hop, hum, jam, kid, mad, met, mom, pen, ran, sad, sit, sun, top.*

## R-Controlled Vowels
When a vowel is followed by the letter *r*, its sound is changed by the *r*. Words with *r*-controlled vowels include: *card, curl, dirt, farm, girl, herd, horn, jerk, torn, turn.*

## Long Vowel and Silent E
If a word has a vowel followed by a consonant and an *e*, usually the vowel is long and the *e* is silent. Long vowels are pronounced the same way as their alphabet names. Words with a long vowel and silent *e* include: *bake, cute, dive, game, home, kite, mule, page, pole, ride, vote.*

## Double Vowels
When two vowels are side by side, usually the first vowel is long and the second vowel is silent. Words with double vowels include: *boat, clean, gray, loaf, meet, neat, paint, pie, play, rain, sleep, tried.*

## Diphthongs
Sometimes when two vowels (or a vowel and a consonant) are side by side, they combine to make a diphthong—a sound that is different from long or short vowel sounds. Diphthongs are: *au/aw, ew, oi/oy, ou/ow.* Words with diphthongs include: *auto, brown, claw, flew, found, join, toy.*

## Double Consonants
When two identical consonants appear side by side, one of them is silent. Words with double consonants include: *bell, fuss, mess, mitt, puff, tall, yell.*

## Consonant Blends
When two or more different consonants are side by side, they usually blend to make a combined sound. Words with consonant blends include: *bent, blob, bride, club, crib, drop, flip, frog, gift, glare, grip, help, jump, mask, most, pink, plane, ring, send, skate, sled, spin, steep, swim, trap, twin.*

## Consonant Digraphs
Sometimes when two different consonants are side by side, they make a digraph that represents a single new sound. Consonant digraphs are: *ch, sh, th, wh*. Words with digraphs include: *bath, chest, lunch, sheet, think, whip, wish*.

## Silent Consonants
Sometimes when two different consonants are side by side, one of them is silent. Words with silent consonants include: *back, dumb, knit, knot, lamb, sock, walk, wrap, wreck*.

## Sight Words
Sight words are those words that a reader must learn to recognize immediately—by sight—instead of by sounding them out. They occur with high frequency in easy texts. Sight words include: *a, am, an, and, as, at, be, big, but, can, come, do, for, get, give, have, he, her, his, I, in, is, it, just, like, look, make, my, new, no, not, now, old, one, out, play, put, red, run, said, see, she, so, some, soon, that, the, then, there, they, to, too, two, under, up, us, very, want, was, we, went, what, when, where, with, you*.

## Exceptions to the "Rules"
Although much of the English language is phonically regular, there are many words that don't follow the above guidelines. For example, a particular combination of letters can represent more than one sound. Double *oo* can represent a long *oo* sound, as in words such as *boot, cool,* and *moon*; or it can represent a short *oo* sound, as in words such as *foot, good,* and *hook*. The letters *ow* can represent a diphthong, as in words such as *brow, fowl,* and *town*; or they can represent a long *o* sound, as in words such as *blow, snow,* and *tow*. Additionally, some high-frequency words such as *some, come, have,* and *said* do not follow the guidelines at all, and *ough* appears in such different-sounding words as *although, enough,* and *thought*.

The phonic guidelines provided in this book are just that—guidelines. They do not cover all the irregularities in our rich and varied language, but are intended to correspond roughly to the phonic lessons taught in the the first and second grades. Phonics provides the foundation for learning to read. Repetition, visual clues, context, and sheer experience provide the rest.